Don't Be a
Chicken

Written by Binks
Illustrated by Ruby Begonia

LOST
COAST
PRESS

Lost Coast Press
155 Cypress Street
Fort Bragg, CA 95437
(800) 773-7782
www.cypresshouse.com

Book and Cover design by Mike Brechner/Cypress House
Cover and Book Illustrations by Ruby Begonia

ISBN: 978-1-935448-22-8
LCCN: 2012941719
Printed in China
2 4 6 8 9 7 5 3 1

Summary:
Hatched by a loving chicken from an egg found abandoned, Gander the goose grows
to demonstrate bravery and independence, inspiring his fearful adoptive family and
encouraging a spirit of adventure for the read-aloud-to-me audience.

This book is dedicated to
Candalaria School in Salem, Oregon,
where strong academic foundations are built.

About Aunt Sissy

Don't Be a Chicken is a story inspired by my sister—"Aunt Sissy"—and her commitment to her wonderful world of animals. Aunt Sissy lives in Salem and attended Candalaria School. Sissy's softness of heart for all animals is easily seen upon visiting her chickens' free range and coop. A portion of the proceeds from the sale of this book will be donated to the Polk County 4H.

Aunt Sissy's chickens were the happiest chickens in the world. They lived on the most beautiful farm in the valley. Their coop was big and warm and clean and safe. Each chicken had her very own nesting box.

Aunt Sissy gave them the very finest chicken feed and table scraps, and they loved the safety of their coop.

Each day, Aunt Sissy would bring her chickens their food and collect their eggs. She did this every day, all year long.

One day while walking by the creek Aunt Sissy found an egg!
She knew it didn't belong to one of her chickens. It was much
too big and too far from the coop. This egg was all alone and
without a mother to care for it.

4

Sissy brought the egg home with her. When she gathered up all the eggs that morning, she put the new egg into Hennie's nesting box, hoping that her chief chicken would keep the egg safe and warm.

Hennie was joyful! She knew that if she took very good care of this new egg, it would make a handsome new chick for her family. She told her sister chickens, "It will be the finest chick you've ever seen."

Just one week later, Hennie felt a rumbling beneath her as she sat on the egg. It was about to hatch—and then out popped the brand-new chick!

He was a healthy, fine-looking chick. He was bigger than most, and he looked different from any other chick the family had ever seen. He had big feet that looked like paddles. His beak was flat like a shovel. Hennie said, "I will call him Gander" (which means *surprise* in chicken talk).

Gander grew quickly, and he began to look even stranger. His feet got bigger. His neck got longer. His beak became even flatter. And Gander didn't act like the other chickens.

One day, when the chickens left their coop to go out and eat, they found Gander splashing about in a big puddle of water. "Come swim with me, and enjoy the sunshine," he called to his family.

The chickens cackled, "Gander, come away from that puddle. You might drown. We don't like to get wet. We only go outside to scratch on the ground and eat. We don't waste our days playing in the sunshine." Then they ran back inside and hid in their nice, safe nesting boxes.

"But there are good things to eat right here," Gander said. There are water bugs and worms. There are tasty roots in the mud. Try some." Gander stuck his shovel-shaped beak deep into the mud.

The chickens were too scared to watch Gander's strange ways.
They just locked the door to their nice, safe coop and closed the
curtains. They didn't even let Gander back inside till it was time
to go to sleep.

That night, when all the chickens were snug in their nests, Gander unlocked the door and stepped outside. He looked all around, and then he shouted, "Wake up! Come out and look at the moon and all the stars."

His shouts woke all the chickens. They quickly covered their eyes. "We never go out at night," they said. "We are afraid of the night and all the things in it. We could be eaten!" Feeling sad for his family, Gander slowly walked back inside the coop.

The next day, as the chickens scratched about, they heard a
bark. It was Josie, Aunt Sissy's dog. The chickens were afraid!
"Run and hide," said Hennie. "Save yourselves!" All the
chickens bumped into each other as they ran like the wind back
into their nice, safe coop. The air outside was filled with dust
and feathers.

But Gander didn't run. "We must guard our home," he said.
As his chicken family peeked out from the safety of the coop,
Gander stood tall. He stuck out his neck and spread his wings.
Then he walked right up to Josie and hissed at her. Gander
looked so big and fierce that Josie ran away.

That night, still shaking in fear of the little dog, the chickens thanked Gander for his bravery. "Your wings are so much bigger than ours," they said. "Soon they will help me fly," Gander said.

A few days later, as the chicken family marched out of their coop to eat, they heard a honking sound from above. "Come and fly with me. The view is wonderful," Gander said. He flapped his wings and flew high into the sky. Afraid that they were seeing a hawk, the chickens ran and hid under the shed.

Gander landed on the puddle and called to his family. They came out of their hiding place very slowly and said, "Gander, if you fly, you might break your bones." Gander replied, "The days are growing colder, and I must get ready to fly to a warmer place far to the south." The chickens could not bear to hear this. They covered their heads with their wings.

Gander practiced for days. Again and again he flapped his wings and flew and sailed and landed. Aunt Sissy packed a sack of treats for Gander to eat on his trip: corn and wheat and all his favorite bugs and roots.

When Gander was ready to leave, Aunt Sissy brought him his sack of food and said, "Good luck, Gander. Be sure to come back in the spring." Gander said, "Thank you for being my friend. Thank you for our wonderful family." Hennie stood on her tippy-toes and hugged Gander with her wings. "Have a safe flight, dear," she said. "You have made life so exciting for us. Before you go, can you tell me, please, how I can make my life more like yours?

"That's easy," Gander said, as his webbed feet left the ground.

"Don't be a Chicken!"

A Kid-friendly Omelet

You'll need:

An adult to help you

3 eggs at room temperature

1 tablespoon of unsalted butter

Salt and pepper, to taste

Warm an 8-inch nonstick frying pan on medium heat.

Crack the eggs into a bowl and beat them with a fork so they break up and mix. Raise the heat to medium-high and drop the butter into the pan. It should bubble and sizzle, but not turn brown. Season the eggs with a little salt and pepper, and pour them into the pan.

Let the eggs bubble slightly for a few seconds, then use a wooden spatula to gently pull the mixture in from the sides of the pan a few times so it gathers in folds in the middle. Leave for a few seconds, and then stir lightly to mix any uncooked egg with the cooked part. Leave for a few seconds again, and then stir a bit faster. Stop while there's some barely cooked egg left.

With the pan flat on the heat, shake it back and forth a few times to settle the mixture. It should slide easily in the pan and look soft and moist on top.

Hold the handle underneath, tilt the pan down and away from you, and let the omelet slide to the edge. With your spatula, fold over the half nearest to you, and tip the omelet onto a plate.

About the Author
and Illustrator

Both the author and the illustrator attended Candalaria Elementary School. Binks lives in northern California, and his sister, Ruby Begonia, lives in Salem, Oregon. Their interests include a tree nursery, organic gardening, art, and all things outdoors. They have degrees in architecture, biology, and medicine.

Don't Be a Chicken was written to reflect Ruby Begonia's love of this earth and all its animals. All profits from the first printing of this book will be given to the Candalaria Elementary School library, after which a portion of all proceeds from sales will go to the Polk County 4H.